MW00762748

LOUIE'S
Saxophone

By Trevor J. Boehm

Text & Illustrations by Trevor J. Boehm

© 2010 Leslie Boehm
All Rights reserved. Except for brief quotation embodied in critical articles and reviews, no part of this book may be reproduced or transmitted in any form or by any means, electronic or mechanical, including photocopying, microfilming, and recording, or by any information storage and retrieval system, without permission in writing from the publisher.

CURRENT PRINTING
10 9 8 7 6 5 4 3 2 1

Library of Congress Cataloging – in Publication Data
Boehm, Trevor J
Louie's Saxophone by Trevor J. Boehm. 24p. cm.
Summary: Louis, a vocally challenged canary, learns another way to make music.
ISBN: 978-1-4507-0822-7
1. Juvenile Literature. I. Boehm, Trevor J. II. Title.

Printed and bound in USA.

For information, contact Leslie Boehm at www.louiessaxophone.com

Part of the proceeds of this book will be donated to charities supporting families living with bipolar and other related disorders.

This book is dedicated to the kids Trevor loved.

  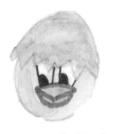

Shannon and Josh's kids:

His nephews and niece - George, Henry, Teddy, Johnny, and Coley

Gretchen's kids:

Samantha, Caleb, Logan, and Ellaray

Acknowledgements

We would like to thank our neighbors and friends, Mary and Regan Stern. Having written two books, Mary had already navigated the self-publishing field. She willingly shared her expertise. The project plan she prepared for us identified specific tasks and suggested deadlines helping us stay on track. Information about her books, *Where Did All the Animals Go?* and *Country Critters*, can be found at www.cowboydogseries.com. We encourage you to take a peek. These books make for great reading with kids!

Regan, our ever-ready 'tech support', scanned the book and began spending long hours (often in the middle of the night) doing the necessary tweaking and fine tuning of each page. When he discovered the Clone feature in Photoshop, it was one of those wonderful 'Aha' moments as his tweaking time was substantially reduced. With Regan's help we were also able to create a font using Trevor's handwriting. Trevor's story and quotes took on even more of his personality when read in his own hand. (Note: This newly created font is called TrevorJBoehm and is available for your use. It can be found at www.louiessaxophone.com). While the project continued it was clear the title of tech support did not adequately describe the multitude of tasks performed by Regan. He became designer, artist and truly the project leader (but we didn't want to tell him at the time). Working closely with each page and the project as a whole, Regan discovered the symbolism of Trevor's color choices and other subtleties Trevor had woven into his book. Sharing these with me reminded me all over again what a creative and gifted person Trevor was and what an insightful, caring and committed man Regan is. We thank you for making this project a reality and especially for appreciating who the author was.

Our project became a family affair for the Sterns as well when their daughter and son-in-law, Elizabeth and Jeremy Hageman, encouraged us to create the website and provided their expertise and support to make it happen.

Without these people it is doubtful Trevor's book would have come to fruition in its current and, we think, pretty classy form. We are grateful for their labor of love and think Trevor would be too!

Darnell and Leslie Boehm
Fall 2010

Remembrance

Puppet shows,
"camping trips" in the family basement,
or meandering around Breckenridge pretending to be French
Trevor was the king of, "Trying to find another way to make music."

He had a somewhat "Peter Pan" approach to life – fun loving and adventurous, but with a gentle spirit that never failed to brighten my day. And though Trevor was 7 years my junior, he had a wisdom that could touch another's soul. Perhaps this came from his high flying adventures - on stage and off. Or perhaps the wisdom came from that gentle place in him that was born of his struggle to find another way to make music.

Thank you for watching 10 hours of my Egyptian home videos — just to make your Big Sis smile. I love you Trev!

Ali

My beloved brother, Trevor Jon, wrote this book. Much like Louis, Trevor was forced to embrace challenges that most of us never face. And yet, the notes that flowed from his gentle and determined spirit created beautiful music. Trevor's heart is on display for the world to enjoy in this book. May his sweet, melodious spirit live on for generations.

I love and miss you, Trevor! Thank you for the thoughtful and touching gift of your book.

Brittany

There was once a canary
named Louie.

Louie was unlike most canaries.
He could not sing. He could not
make any noise at all.

While all the other canaries were bought from the pet store, Louie was not. This made Louie very sad.

"Nobody wants a silent canary," thought Louie.
"I should just run away!"

That night, when the pet store was closed,
Louie flew from the shop.

While in the park, Louie saw the most beautiful bird he had ever seen. She was singing with the voice of an angel.

"Hey there," said the bird.
"I'm Robin. What's your name?"

Louie could only write his name on a
scrap of paper. He hung his head sadly.
Louie wished he could sing too.

Louie blew into the saxophone. He made one long note. He blew again. Soon he had learned to play an entire song.

Eventually, Louie and Robin started a band and played for anyone who wished to hear them.

The two fell in love and began a family.
They couldn't be happier.
Louie can, at long last, make music, with some
creativity and a little help from his saxophone.

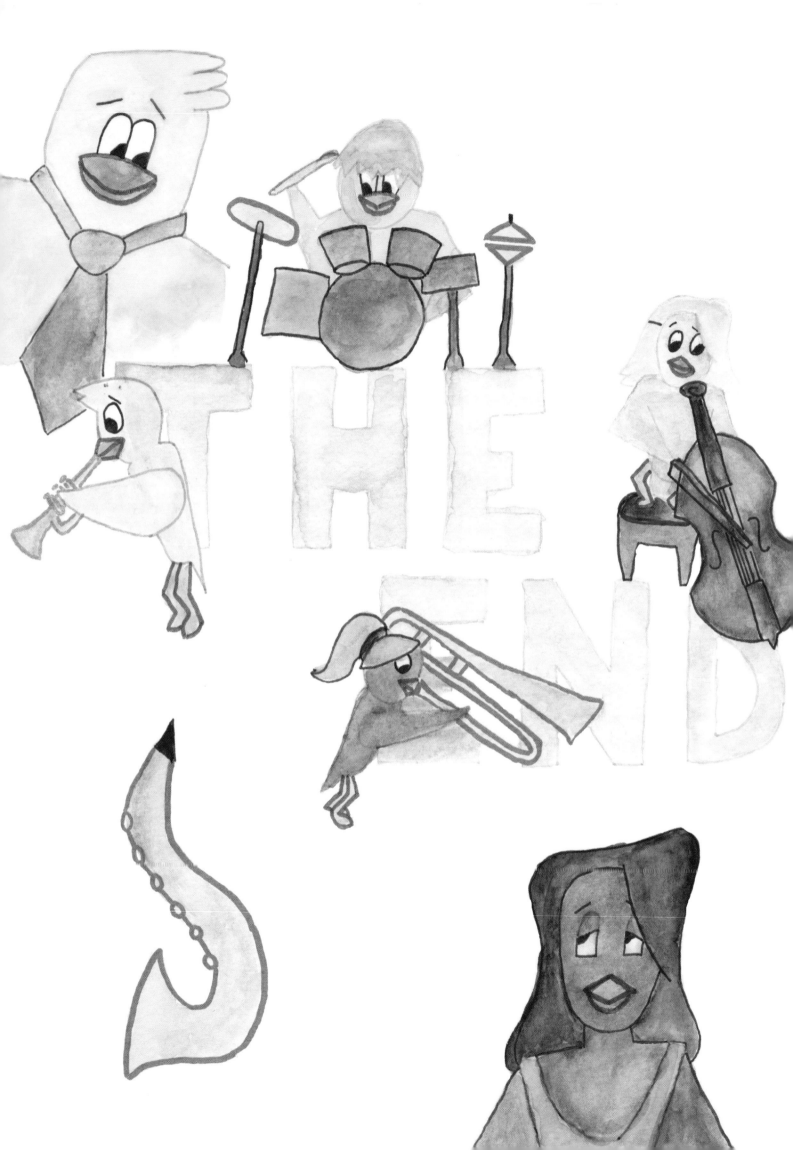

"People would be better off abandoning their goal of being 'normal' and instead learn to excel in their God-given talents."

"I want to help others see their dreams by inspiring them as I accomplish my own dreams."

Trevor J. Boehm

Facing page:

Self-Portrait
Collage
2005
(Pieces cut from magazines)